By Mary Man-Kong • Based on the original screenplay by Cliff Ruby & Elana Lesser

Special thanks to Vicki Jaeger, Monica Okazaki, Rob Hudnut, Shelley Dvi-Vardhana, Jesyca C. Durchin, Shea Wageman, Jennifer Twiner McCarron, Trevor Wyatt, Greg Richardson, Derek Goodfellow, Genevieve Lacombe, Theresa Johnston, Michael Douglas, David Pereira, Jonathon Busby, Sean Newton, Zoe Evamy, Steve Lumley, Arnie Roth, and Walter P. Martishius

## A Random House PICTUREBACK® Book
### Random House 🏠 New York

Library of Congress Control Number: 2005937748    ISBN-13: 978-0-375-83762-3    ISBN-10: 0-375-83762-0
www.randomhouse.com/kids    Printed in the United States of America    10 9

Once upon a time, there was a kind king who had twelve beautiful daughters. The king raised the princesses as best he could, but he needed help.

"I love them," the king said to himself. "But at times I don't understand them."

Each of the princesses had a different hobby, but they *all* loved one thing . . .

. . . dancing! Princess Genevieve especially loved to dance. Every
day she and her sisters would practice their leaps and twirls in
the palace garden. The royal cobbler, Derek, would often bring
the princesses new dancing shoes and mend their old ones.
    Derek was secretly in love with Princess Genevieve.

Knowing that the raising of his daughters called for a woman's touch, the king asked his cousin, Duchess Rowena, to come live in the castle. Rowena wanted to be queen, so she plotted to slowly poison the king. But first she had to pretend to help with the girls' upbringing.

"You must learn to be proper princesses," Rowena declared as she took away their beautiful gowns and playthings—and even forbade them to dance!

The triplets were especially upset because it was their birthday. "We always danced on our birthdays when Mother was alive," Lacey complained.

To cheer them up, the other princesses gave each of the triplets a copy of their mother's favorite book, *The Dancing Princess*. "She had one made for each of us with our favorite flower on the cover," explained Ashlyn.

Everyone listened quietly as Genevieve read the story about a princess who danced on special stones, revealing a hidden magical world.

Suddenly, Lacey stumbled and her book landed on a stone with the same flower painted on it!

"It's just like in Mother's story!" exclaimed Courtney. The sisters quickly matched their books to the different stones.

"In the story, the princess danced on the stones to find the magical world," Genevieve added. As the princesses gracefully danced from stone to stone, a bell chimed. On the last stone, Genevieve twirled three times. Suddenly, the stone sank down, revealing a set of stairs leading to . . .

. . . the most beautiful place they had ever seen! Silver trees and jeweled flowers surrounded a golden pavilion with musical instruments.

"I wish there was music," Genevieve whispered. With those words, a diamond flower sprinkled magic dust on the instruments—and they began to play! The princesses leaped and twirled to the music.

"Ouch!" Lacey exclaimed as she tripped and scraped her knee. "Why can't I be good at something?"

"Mother always told us, big or small, there's a difference only you can make," Genevieve gently told her sister. She dipped her handkerchief in the sparkling lake and dabbed her little sister's knee. Amazingly, the scrape disappeared!

The sisters danced well into the night before they returned to their bedroom. And the next morning, all twelve princesses were so tired that they couldn't stay awake! Rowena was getting very suspicious by the time Derek arrived to fix their shoes.

"It looks like someone's been having a good time," Derek said as he polished and mended the princesses' worn shoes.

"We did," Genevieve said as she danced the steps from the night before. "But I don't trust Rowena. Will you find out what she's up to?"

"I'll do my best," the cobbler promised.

Meanwhile, Rowena was convinced
that the princesses had sneaked out
and danced all night with princes.
So that evening, the duchess ordered
her henchman, Desmond, to guard
the princesses' bedroom door and
make sure they didn't leave. But as
soon as he fell asleep, Genevieve and
her sisters sneaked back to the
golden pavilion.

The girls laughed and danced
with beautiful paper fans until the
soles of their shoes were worn
through again.

Soon Derek discovered Rowena's plot to become queen. He rushed to the princesses' bedroom to tell Genevieve, but they were all missing. Remembering Genevieve's dance steps, Derek stepped on the stones—and found Genevieve in the enchanted world!

But Rowena had secretly followed Derek to the magic pavilion. There she came up with a wicked plan. She picked two of the enchanted flowers and returned to the princesses' bedroom. Then Rowena smashed all the magic stones. The princesses were trapped in the golden pavilion!

"I wish to know the way out," Genevieve said. Instantly, the jeweled flowers sprinkled magic dust on special stones. "May I have this dance?" Derek asked. As Genevieve and Derek danced across the stones together, a staircase appeared for their escape!

Derek and the princesses rushed to the palace. Realizing she was cornered, Rowena held up one of the magic flowers. "I wish for armor to protect the queen," she said. Instantly, a suit of armor came to life! Thinking quickly, Derek grabbed the fireplace poker and smashed the armor to pieces.

"I wish you would dance your life away," Rowena shouted, using her last enchanted flower. Magic dust blew toward Genevieve and Derek, but Genevieve quickly flipped open her paper fan and blew the dust right back toward the duchess. "Help! Help!" Rowena cried as her feet danced her far away from the castle.

With Rowena finally gone, the sisters had to save their father. The poison had begun to work and the king was very ill.

"I think I can help," Lacey said. She gave her father some water from her vial. "It's from the lake. I took some after I scraped my knee."

Slowly, the king's eyes fluttered open and he smiled at his daughters.

"It worked!" Genevieve exclaimed.

"Where would I be without you?" the king asked his littlest daughter. "Your mother always told me . . ."

"Big or small, there's a difference only you can make," finished Lacey with a smile.

"And you all have made a difference," the king said to his daughters.

That spring, a beautiful wedding took place at the palace. Everyone came to celebrate the marriage of Derek and Princess Genevieve—and they all danced the night away.